To Brian and Sue, for all your help –PB
To Nona –MM

American edition published in 2012 by Andersen Press USA, an imprint of Andersen Press Ltd. www.andersenpressusa.com
Distributed in the United States and Canada by Lerner Publishing Group, Inc. • 241 First Avenue North • Minneapolis, MN 55401 U.S.A. www.lernerbooks.com

Text copyright © Peter Bently, 2011. Illustration copyright © Mei Matsuoka, 2011.

First published in Great Britain in 2011 by Andersen Press Ltd., 20 Vauxhall Bridge Road, London SW1V 2SA.

Library of Congress Cataloging-in-Publication Data available.

Colour separated in Switzerland by Photolitho AG, Zürich. Printed and bound in Singapore by Tien Wah Press.

ISBN: 978-0-7613-8990-3 • 1 – TWP – 12/31/11

The Great Sheep Shenanigans

Peter Bently & Mei Matsuoka

ANDERSEN PRESS USA

"A lamb for my supper will taste mighty fine!"
Thought a wily old wolf by the name of Lou Pine
As he sneakily, slyly snuck up on the flock—
But it wasn't the sheep who were in for a shock.

He chuckled,
"How stunningly cunning I am!"

As he slunk through the hedge and met . . .

Rambo the Ram.

"Scram!" bellowed Rambo.

"Vamoose!   Steer clear!

Wolves are NOT welcome!

Buzz off out of here!"

"What I need," grumbled Lou, "is a sheepy disguise
To give those dumb muttons a nasty surprise!"

So he wrapped himself up in a fluffy white gown . . .

. . . that belonged to Ma Watson, the best shot in town.

He lay on the road . . .

. . . to get covered in gunk.

"Baa-ha!" laughed the sheep. "It's an overgrown skunk!"

At the fair, Lou saw cotton candy on a stick.

"My own candy fleece! What a fabulous trick!"

He flicked on the switch, and at first it was fun,

But faster
and **faster** and
FASTER

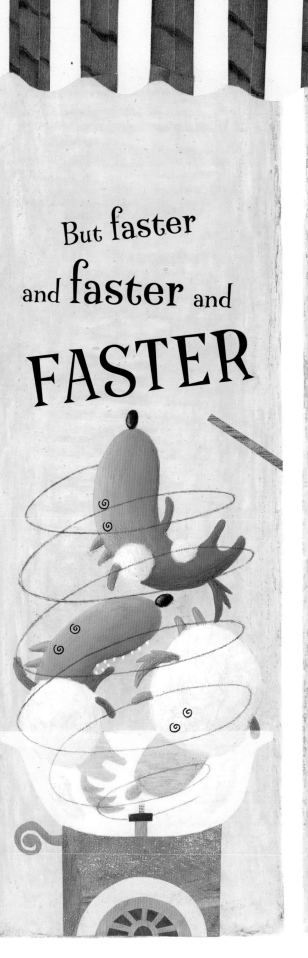

he spun . . .

He looked in the mirror
and felt his heart sink.
He'd ended up dizzy

and sticky
and PINK!

Lou found a thicket of blossoming trees.

Down came the blossoms

and down came the bees!

"I know!" spluttered Lou.
"I've a brilliant plan!
It's time for a trip to
Red Riding Hood's gran!"

"Hello, Granny dearest! It's me, Little Red!"
"My word, what a **big ball** of yarn!" Granny said.

Lou dropped his hood and declared, "All the better
For you to get cracking and knit me a sweater!
And if it's not done by the time I get back,
I'll be in the mood for a Gran-flavored snack!"

The very next day Lou returned for a fitting
And had to admit Gran was dandy at knitting.
He chuckled, "How smashingly dashing I am!

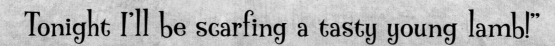
Tonight I'll be scarfing a tasty young lamb!"

But Gran thought,
"He'll pay me for knitting that woolly!
I'll play my own trick on that nasty big bully!"
While Lou wasn't looking, she grabbed a loose thread

And tied it at once to the end of her bed . . .

As he slipped through the hedgerow, some ewes standing near

Looked up at old Lou and said, "Morning, my dear!

Can you check on our lambs? They're behind that big tree."

"No problem," said Lou. "You can leave them to me!"

"I fooled them!" thought Lou. "What a genius I am!

Now shall I have cutlets? Or roast leg of lamb?

Or chops and mint sauce? Or even lamb stew?

Or burgers? Moussaka? Or lamb vindaloo?"

He hungrily hurried as far as the tree
And peered all about, but no lambs could he see.
"They must be here somewhere. They can't have gone far.

Come out, little lambkins, wherever you are!"

And then he heard footsteps.

"Aha! Here's a lamb!"

So Lou looked around and saw . . .

Rambo
the Ram.

He aimed his big horns at the wolf's derriere

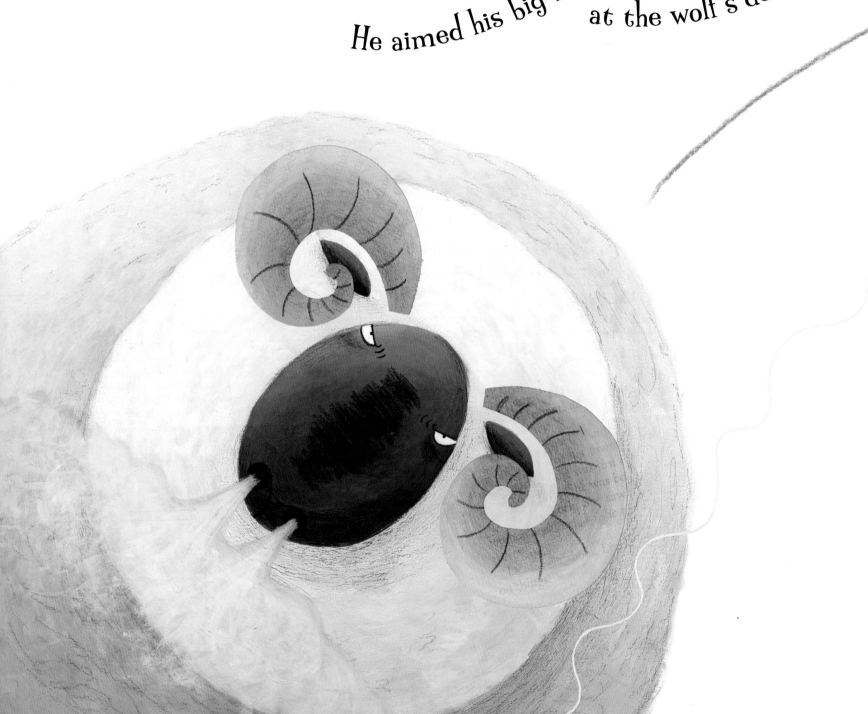

And sent him skedaddling up in the air.

"Ouch!
My behind!"
howled Lou as he flew…

And landed **kersplat**

in a big pile of **poo!**

"I think that's the last of the wolf and his wiles,"
Laughed Rambo. "From now on we'll smell him for miles!"